CLAUDE

at the Beach

lex T. Smith

For my Dad,
Master of the Terrible Joke

Ω
PEACHTREE PUBLISHERS
1700 Chattahoochee Avenue
Atlanta, Georgia 30318-2112
www.peachtree-online.com

Text and illustrations © 2011 by Alex T. Smith

First published in the United Kingdom in 2011 by Hodder Children's Books
First United States version published in 2014 by Peachtree Publishers
First United States trade paperback edition published in 2016

Artwork created digitally. Title is hand lettered; text is typeset in Italian Garamond BT.

Printed and bound in November 2015 in China by RR Donnelley Asia Printing Solutions Lir

10 9 8 7 6 5 4 3 2 1 (hardcover)
10 9 8 7 6 5 4 3 2 1 (trade paperback)

Library of Congress Cataloging-in-Publication Data

Smith, Alex T.
  Claude at the beach / by Alex T. Smith.
      pages cm
  Summary: When Claude the dog and his friend, Sir Bobblysock, decide to have a
vacation at the beach, Claude rescues a man from a shark, Sir Bobblysock wins a sand
sculpting contest, and both go in search of pirate treasure.
ISBN: 978-1-56145-703-8 (hardcover)
ISBN: 978-1-56145-919-3 (trade paperback)
  [1. Dogs—Fiction. 2. Socks—Fiction. 3. Beaches—Fiction. 4. Humorous stories.] I.
Title.
  PZ7.S6422Ckh 2014
  [E]—dc23
                                        2013032152

CLAUDE

at the Beach

ALEX T. SMITH

PEACHTREE
ATLANTA

Chapter 1

At 112 Waggy Avenue, behind a
tall front door with a big brass
knocker, lives Claude.

And here he is now.

Claude is a dog.
Claude is a small dog.
Claude is a small,
plump dog.

Claude is a small,
plump dog who
wears a beret and
a lovely red sweater.

5

Claude lives in his house with two
people who are too tall to fit on this
page. They are called Mr. and Mrs.
Shinyshoes, and they both have very
shiny shoes and neat ankles.

Every morning while Claude is still
tucked in his bed, Mr. and Mrs.
Shinyshoes whiz around the house,
getting ready to go to work.

7

Sometimes Claude watches them with his beady eyes and sometimes he just pretends to be asleep.

Then at half past eight
on the dot, Mr. and Mrs.
Shinyshoes put on their
coats. "Be a good boy, Claude,"
they say. "We'll see you later!"
And off they go to work.

Once the front door has closed behind them, Claude leaps out of bed. He puts his beret on his head and fishes his best friend, Sir Bobblysock, out from under the blankets. It is time for an adventure!

Sir Bobblysock

Where will Claude and
Sir Bobblysock go next?

11

Chapter 2

One morning, Claude had a brilliant idea. "I think I will go on vacation!" he said.

Sir Bobblysock decided he would come, too, as he had been very busy lately and wanted a rest.

Claude had never been on vacation before, so he didn't know quite what he was supposed to do. He thought it would be a good idea to take all sorts of interesting and useful things with him, just in case they came in handy.

So he pulled out a suitcase from under his bed and started to pack.

He put in some underpants and a tambourine. He added some sunscreen and some whipped cream in a can. He threw in a lampshade, some sticky tape, and a selection of slightly squished sandwiches.

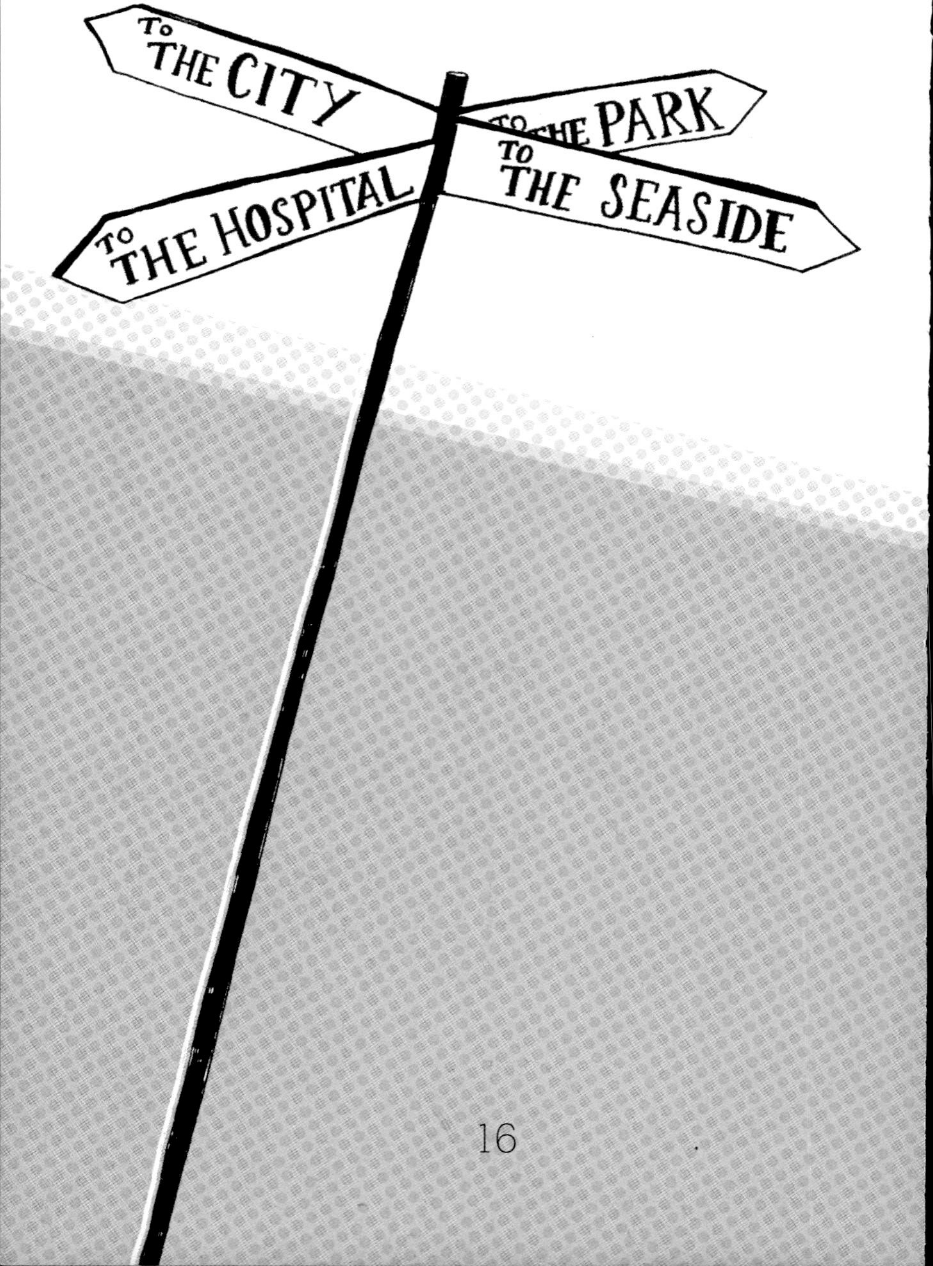
TO THE CITY
TO THE PARK
TO THE HOSPITAL
TO THE SEASIDE

Then Claude clicked his suitcase
closed and set off for the beach,
with Sir Bobblysock hopping along
behind him.

It was very busy at the beach. There were people sunbathing and sitting in deck chairs, and children shouting and playing all over the place. Everyone seemed to be in their underwear!

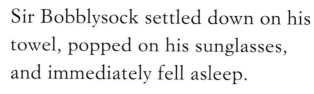

Sir Bobblysock settled down on his towel, popped on his sunglasses, and immediately fell asleep.

Claude thought he had better try to fit in too. He opened up his suitcase, took out the pair of underpants he'd packed, and pulled them on.

Unfortunately, the underpants belonged to Mr. Shinyshoes, so they were much too big for Claude!

He stood scratching his head for a moment, wondering how to keep them up, before he remembered he'd packed some sticky tape.

Ah, that was better.

23

It was a lovely sunny day. Claude wanted to get a tan, but he knew that the hot sun could burn him if he wasn't careful. And although he liked the color pink, he would clash dreadfully with the wallpaper back at home if he got burned.

24

Along the beach he saw a man
squirting cream all over himself.
Claude thought he would copy
him. He got out his sunscreen and
his whipped cream and set to work.

25

First, he covered himself in sunscreen from the tip of his nose to the toes of his sensible shoes. He rubbed it in very carefully. Then he gave the can of whipped cream a quick shake. He squeezed out a big frothy dollop of cream on top of his beret.

Now Claude was ready to start
having fun.

While he was strutting up and down
the beach in his new swimming
trunks, he heard a shout from
somewhere out at sea.

Claude spun around and squinted
in the direction of the noise.
He gasped!

A man was splashing wildly around
in the water—and just behind him
was an enormous shark!

Chapter 3

Claude looked around to see where the lifeguard was. He and Sir Bobblysock had seen programs on television about emergencies like this. He knew a lifeguard should be diving into the water to help.

But the lifeguard wasn't. He was helping
somebody with her beach balls.

Claude rolled his eyes. Calmly, he reached under his beret, found his floaties, and popped them on his arms. Then he dashed toward the water and jumped into the waves.

Claude had won awards for his dog paddle, so it didn't take him long to get to the scene of the emergency.

Claude tapped the
enormous shark on the
fin and cleared his throat.
"It is not very nice to eat
people," he said. "A juicy bone
baguette is much more delicious."

And he took his emergency
bone baguette out from
under his beret.

The shark looked very surprised.
Then the shark looked very pleased
indeed. He took the juicy bone
baguette gently in his gigantic teeth
and swam off, as happy as anything.

"Hold on to my tail please,"
Claude said to the
man, and together
they dog-paddled
back to shore.

Everyone on the beach had been
watching very closely, and they were
all amazed by Claude's bravery.
When Claude arrived back on the
shore with the rescued man, they
cheered.

"HOORAY!" they cried.

Everyone except Sir Bobblysock,
because he was still fast asleep
on his towel.

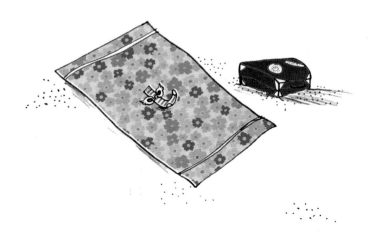

Chapter 4

All that excitement made Claude feel a bit peckish. It was nearly eleven o'clock, after all.

Usually he and Sir Bobblysock had a nice cup of tea and a jam tart for their snack. But since he was on vacation today, Claude wanted something more exotic—like an ice cream, perhaps.

He woke up Sir Bobblysock with
a prod, and together they strolled
to the shop.

The shop was full of French people who had come to the beach for their vacation.

They were all speaking French.

Oh! Un petit chien!
Oh! A little dog!

Of course! thought Claude. *On vacation, you have to speak another language.*

So Claude decided to copy them. He pulled out his phrase book from under his beret and asked for two ice creams in what he hoped was French.

The shopkeeper didn't seem to understand, so Claude tried again— more loudly this time.

Excusez-moi, 'ave you une glace à flavor of juicy bone?

Claude hoped this meant *Excuse me, do you have any juicy bone flavor ice cream?*

The man behind the counter was utterly perplexed and decided to just give Claude three enormous ice creams, an inner tube, and a large flag, all for free!

Claude and Sir Bobblysock left the shop slurping their ice creams, feeling very pleased with themselves.

49

Once they had finished their midmorning treats, Claude wondered what else they could do on the beach. He looked around and saw some children making sand castles.

It looked rather fun so he decided to make his own. Sir Bobblysock joined in too.

After about an hour, Claude had finished his sand castle. He was very pleased with it.

He looked over at Sir Bobblysock's effort.

"Some people are dreadful
show-offs," Claude sniffed.

Then he noticed someone with a
clipboard looking carefully at all
the sand castles. She stared at
Sir Bobblysock's for a long time.

It turned out they had entered
a sand castle competition without
even knowing it—and Sir Bobblysock
won first prize! It was a pair of
snazzy flip-flops! Claude put them
under his beret for safety.

Chapter 5

Claude and Sir Bobblysock were resting on their towel when they saw some interesting-looking people stumping along the sand toward them.

"Arrrrrrrrrrrrr!" cried their leader, licking a popsicle. "We be looking to look for some treasure, so we be!" And he flapped a treasure map at Claude. "Will you help us, matey? I be Porthole Pete, I be, and this be my crew, Slopbucket Stu and Deadeye Denise."

Sir Bobblysock, who knew about these things, thought that they might be pirates.

But Claude thought looking for treasure sounded fun, so he nodded politely, packed up his suitcase, and followed Porthole Pete to the dock.

A piratey-looking ship, *The Damp Dog*, was bobbing around in the waves.

Sir Bobblysock was very doubtful about the whole idea. In the past, he had suffered badly from seasickness—but he followed Claude anyway.

The treasure map showed there was an enormous chest full of goodies hidden nearby on Skull Island.

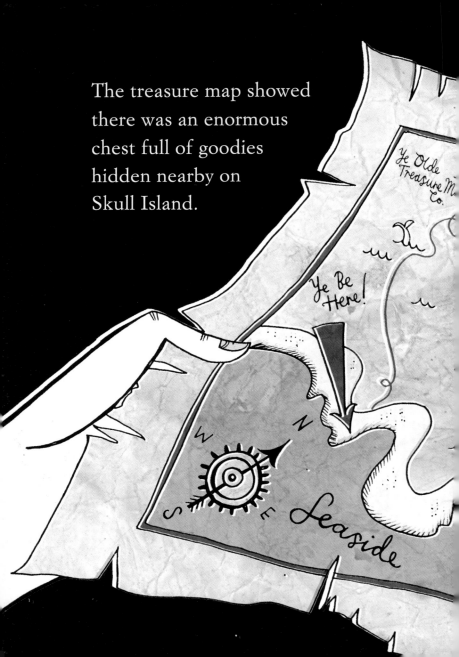

Claude and the pirates sailed along at a terrific pace. Sir Bobblysock found the sea rather unsettling. He spent most of the time lying down in a cabin with cucumber slices over his eyes.

Then they arrived at the island and began looking for the treasure.

Claude, Sir Bobblysock, and the pirates looked

under rocks,

around palm trees,

and down holes, but the
treasure was nowhere to be seen.

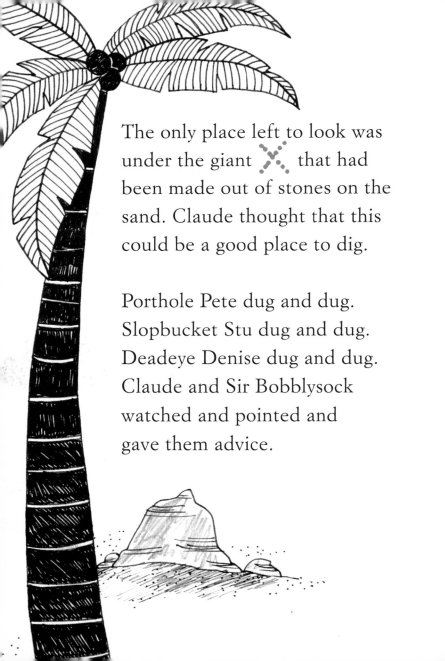

The only place left to look was under the giant ✗ that had been made out of stones on the sand. Claude thought that this could be a good place to dig.

Porthole Pete dug and dug. Slopbucket Stu dug and dug. Deadeye Denise dug and dug. Claude and Sir Bobblysock watched and pointed and gave them advice.

Finally, there was a deafening *clang!*
which gave Sir Bobblysock
a headache and made Claude's
ears wobble.

Claude and Sir Bobblysock looked into the deep, dark hole...

"HOORAY!" they cried.

They had found the treasure!

Quickly, they pulled the chest out of the sand and scampered back toward their ship with it. But they hadn't gone very far before they heard a cry!

74

Chapter 6

"Oh no!" shouted Porthole Pete. "'Tis Naughty Nora, the fearsome naughty pirate, and all her naughty crew! Run!"

So Claude, Sir Bobblysock, and the crew of *The Damp Dog* started to run, but...

UH-OH! Claude tripped.

They were caught.

Claude started to feel a bit sweaty
under his collar. Sir Bobblysock
could feel his heart beating
in his ears.

Naughty Nora strutted up to
Claude's suitcase and had
a good snoop inside.

She looked at the lampshade.
She looked at the tambourine.
She looked at the whipped cream.

"Hmm...," she said.

"Captain?" said one of the naughty pirates. "Don't we need a new lampshade for our ship, 'cause you wore our last one as a hat and then we lost it?"

Naughty Nora nodded slowly.

"And we could do with a new tambourine," said another naughty shipmate, "'cause you used our last one as a tray for afternoon tea and then we lost it."

Naughty Nora nodded again.

"And we could do with some more whipped cream," said the first naughty shipmate, "'cause you took the last can on a picnic and then—"

"Yes, all right!" snapped Naughty Nora.

The other pirates watched silently as Naughty Nora stood frowning, looking from the treasure chest to the suitcase and back again. She sniffed one of the slightly squished sandwiches.

"We will swap you our treasure chest for your suitcase full of interesting and useful things!" she said. "Deal?" And she held out a hand for Claude to shake.

Claude looked at Porthole
Pete and Porthole Pete
looked at Claude.
Then Claude
nodded politely to
Naughty Nora
and shook
her hand.

Chapter 7

Before the naughty pirates could change their minds, Slopbucket Stu had flung the treasure chest on top of his head, and the crew of *The Damp Dog* skedaddled back to their ship.

"Hooray for Claude!" shouted the pirates. "Hip hip, hooray!"

Claude looked at his feet and went a bit red. Sir Bobblysock made a low bow.

"'Ere, matey!" cried Porthole Pete as he opened the chest and plunged his hands into all the gold. "Why don't you and Sir Bobblysock come and join us full time 'ere on *The Damp Dog*? You be makin' great treasure hunters, so you be!"

But Claude was feeling tired—
going on vacation was more exciting
than he had ever imagined. So he
and Sir Bobblysock said their
goodbyes and made their way home
with a beret *full* of treasure.

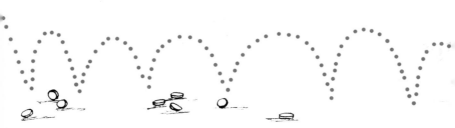

That night when Mr. and Mrs.
Shinyshoes came home from work,
there was sand all over the place.
Mrs. Shinyshoes was sure she could
smell a whiff of seaweed.

"Where on earth has all of this
treasure come from?" asked Mr.
Shinyshoes, biting one of the gold
coins to see if it was real.

"I don't know," said Mrs. Shinyshoes.
"And I'm not even going to ask why
there's a pair of your underpants here,
covered in sand!"

Claude and Sir Bobblysock
pretended to be asleep.
It would be their little secret.

*Keep your eyes open for Claude and Sir Bobblysock.
You never know where they'll turn up next.*

CLAUDE
in the City

A visit to the city is delightful but ordinary until Claude accidentally foils a robbery and heals a whole waiting room full of patients! HC: $12.95 / 978-1-56145-697-0, PB: $7.95 / 978-1-56145-843-1

CLAUDE
at the Circus

An ordinary walk in the park leads to a walk on a tightrope when Claude accidentally joins the circus and becomes the star of the show! HC: $12.95 / 978-1-56145-702-1

CLAUDE
in the Country

When a fearsome bull interrupts Claude's afternoon down on the farm, he must think like a cowboy to save the day! HC: $12.95 / 978-1-56145-918-6

CLAUDE
on the Slopes

Claude loves the Snowy Mountains—but when his winter wonderland threatens to avalanche, he must make a daring rescue! HC: $12.95 / 978-1-56145-805-9

CLAUDE
in the Spotlight

Claude is ready for his stage debut—but when a spooky theater ghost tries to ruin the performance, Claude knows the show must go on! HC: $12.95 / 978-1-56145-895-0

3 1531 00444 1603